Belgium
during World War Two

North Sea

NETHERLANDS

Maas River

Ostend • • Antwerp

BELGIUM

GERMANY

River Schelde
Brussels • Liege

Charleroi
Meuse River

ARDENNES

FRANCE

LaRoche

Anna's Chalet

LUXEMBOURG

U.S.S.R.

IA

Black Sea

IA

TURKEY

The Invasion of Poland
September, 1939

LATVIA

Baltic Sea
LITHUANIA

U

EAST PRUSSIA

S

Poznan
Kutno Warsaw

P O L A N D

S

° Lublin

G
E
R

° Krakow

R

M
A
N
Y

CZECHOSLOVAKIA

HUNGARY

ROMANIA

➤ German Invasion—September 1, 1939

⟩ Russian Invasion—September 17, 1939

Night of Flames